Comings and Goings at

Parrot Park

MARY MURPHY

ILLUSTRATED BY
JESSICA AHLBERG

WALKER
BOOKS

To De   hys

First published 2008 by Walker Books Ltd
87 Vauxhall Walk, London SE11 5HJ

2 4 6 8 10 9 7 5 3 1

Text © 2008 Mary Murphy
Illustrations © 2008 Jessica Ahlberg

The right of Mary Murphy and Jessica Ahlberg to be identified as author
and illustrator respectively of this work has been asserted by them in
accordance with the Copyright, Designs and Patents Act 1988

This book has been typeset in Bembo Educational
and Myriad Tilt Bold

Printed and bound by J. H. Haynes & Co., Ltd., Sparkford

British Library Cataloguing in Publication Data:
a catalogue record for this book is available from the British Library

ISBN 978-1-4063-0220-2

www.walkerbooks.co.uk

Canadian Cousins
7

Jumble Sale
25

The Forever Jumper
45

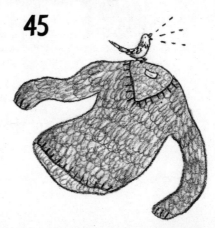

Here are all the Murphys
of 53 Parrot Park, looking at their
photo album.

Rory doing
an experiment

Anna in a tree

Barney with Mary

Cormac and Catherine
in the school play

Susan's first tooth

Mammy and Daddy
on the beach

ORLA

AILEEN

CONOR AND SEÁN

AUNTIE GRACE
AND UNCLE DERMOT

Canadian Cousins

LITTLE NIALL

All the Murphys have cousins in
Canada. This July, for the first time,
these Canadian Murphys are coming
to Ireland. Some of the time they will
stay with all the Murphys.

"We'll have to squash in," says Mammy.

"Sure we have the garden,"
says Daddy.

Daddy shakes a sack empty.
Out come ropes, hooks, stakes
and a bulk of canvas.
"A tent!" says Anna.

"There are two more where
this came from," says Daddy. He
borrowed them from the neighbours.

Tap … thup, thup, thup! goes
Daddy's mallet.

Everyone helps to put up the tents,
except Smarty and Pookie,
the dogs, who only
want to play.

At last three tents stand, like spokes
on a wheel, with a space at the centre.
  "This is going to be great," says Anna.
The camp waits.
All the Murphys wait.
The afternoon ticks on.
A car stops outside.

"Here come the Canadian Murphys,"
says Daddy.

"Seán!" says Dermot.

"Dermot!" says Daddy.

They are brothers, and have not
seen each other for years.

Straight away
the cousins are friends.
The Canadian Murphys
have different accents. But they
talk as loudly, and as much,
as the Dublin
Murphys.

They look like them too,
but with checked shirts and straight
jeans, not shorts and knitted jumpers.
Orla, the one like Mary,
has a baseball cap
with a bear
on it.

The Canadian Murphys love
the camp.

"This is going to be great,"
says Aileen, the one like Anna.

"Can we have a campfire?"
asks Conor, the one like Cormac.

"Yes," answers Cormac. "We just need sticks, and matches."

"Don't mind him," says Rory to Orla. "We're not allowed matches."

"We aren't either," says Orla.

The camp
grows better
and better.
Canadian and
Dublin Murphys collect
sticks for the campfire.

An adult will light it later.

Mary brings dog blankets.

Catherine puts a jar

of flowers at each tent.

Susan and Niall, the

one like Susan, hide in

the hairy blankets.

Rory brings out his budgie, Jacky.

"We could live here," says Anna.

"Yes," says Aileen. "For the whole summer."

Evening comes. Televisions flicker in neighbours' houses.

Uncle Dermot will light the fire.

"First check there isn't a hedgehog," says Mary.

There are no hedgehogs in Canada. There is no hedgehog here now.

"Bears come into our garden sometimes," says Orla.

There are no bears left in Ireland.

"A lion came into ours once," Cormac tells Conor. "We locked him in the shed."

"We did that to a bear," says Conor. "He bashed down the door."

"That's what the lion did too," says Cormac.

The fire cracks in the night.
Susan and Niall sleep.
Tonight Mammy and
Auntie Grace
will stay
indoors
with them.
Tomorrow
they can have
a turn in the tents.

The last of the sticks have burnt.

The tents are open like caves.

Children and dogs squash into two
tents. Daddy and Uncle Dermot sleep
in the third, smallest tent: the first time
they have camped together since
they were little.

The tents are warm and full
of little sounds.

"There's a lion outside," whispers
someone.

Little Seán, the one like Catherine,
goes in to sleep with his daddy.
Catherine goes in to sleep with hers.

Pookie keeps guard. She gets no sleep.

The July days slip by.

The Canadian cousins go home, back to Canada. The borrowed tents go home too, back to their owners.

There is flat grass where the tents sat, and a black patch from the fire. The space is given a new name: it is the part of the garden all the Murphys call the Canadian Camp.

Jumble Sale

"**H**ere, cat-cat-cat!"
calls Anna.
Things are missing in
53 Parrot Park. The cat.
Mammy's keys. Catherine's bracelet.
And yet there are things everywhere.
An interesting, bulky parcel arrives.
More things!

Checked shirts and straight jeans,
passed on from Canada. And there are
Canadian books, and a Canadian tent.

"Bags I the bear cap!" says
Mary quickly.

Now all the Murphys look
like Canadians.

"Where can the tent go?"
Daddy wonders.

He opens the kitchen
press. The cat tumbles
out. FLOOMP!

Also a bicycle pump,
clothes for mending,
skates, a flock of wool
and Squeaky,
the one-eared,
flattish squirrel.

Fifty-three Parrot Park needs a clear-up.
Wool and mending go into bags.
Clothes and toys go on their owners'
beds. Soon the beds are packed, but
there are more clothes and toys.

Outdoor things like skates go in the
garage. Books go on bookshelves.

The shelves are packed, but there are
more books, including the Canadian ones.

"You grow bigger," says Mammy,
"and the house grows smaller."

"We've too much stuff," says Anna.

One of the Murphys has an
idea. A jumble sale.

"This mountainy jigsaw can be in the jumble sale," says Mary.

"And this Action Man," says Anna.

"No broken stuff," says Rory.

"Choo-choo!" sings Susan.
Cormac grumpily
gives her the
broken train.

There is a tower
of comics to sell.

There is a box of liquorice.
All the Murphys hate liquorice.

Catherine's bed is
crowded with soft animal toys.
The oldest is Chichi, the sheep
Catherine has had since she was born.
The newest is Patsy, the rabbit.
They will both stay.
So will Lynne, the sitting-up panda.
Quackie, the yellow duck who was
free with shampoo,
can go.

Also the
scratchy parrot
with no name
can go,
and Piggley
the pig, Smiley
the monkey puppet
and Squeaky, the one-eared,
flattish squirrel.

Catherine chooses
ten. "They'll be fine
together," she says.

Saturday is Jumble Sale Day.

"Fizzy orange!" shouts Anna from the Canadian refreshments tent.

"Flapjacks!" sings Anne Miller, who is helping Anna.

There is a competition. Guess how
many liquorice pieces are in the jar?
The prize is the liquorice.

Cormac runs a raffle for a cowboy
hat.

Catherine minds
the toy stall. Karl Jones
buys a catapult.

"I want this Action Man," says Paul
Lahart. "But I've no money left."

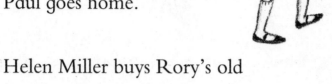

"It's Anna's Action
Man," Catherine tells him.
Paul goes home.

Helen Miller buys Rory's old
binoculars (his new ones are better).

"I'll buy the
box of animals,"
says Geraldine
Baston. "But
I don't want
this dog thing."
She pulls Squeaky
out of the box.
"All or none,"
Catherine says firmly.
"And she's a squirrel."
"I'll buy them all,"
says Anne Miller. "Bonzo
would love that old dog thing."
Bonzo Miller is the Millers' dog.
He would chew Squeaky to bits.

"Wait," says Geraldine. "I'll take
them. I'll give the dog thing to Major."

But Geraldine's dog, Major Baston,
is worse than Bonzo Miller.

Catherine picks up Squeaky.
"I forgot," she says. "Squeaky is not
for sale."

Geraldine buys the other toys. She
will give them a good, new home.

Paul Lahart comes back with
a model rocket to swap with Anna's
Action Man.

Mr Lahart wins the raffle.

"A fine new hat for gardening,"

he says, though it is an old hat.

The jumble sale is over.

43

Fifty-three Parrot Park feels bigger. All the Murphys have some money and some space.

Some of their new stuff was old before, somewhere else. Some of their old stuff is new stuff, somewhere else. And some of their old stuff is still home.

The Forever Jumper

It is September.

School starts tomorrow.

All the Murphys are in Arnott's shop.

"Can I help?" asks the man in charge

of school uniforms. His badge says:

MR O'CONNOR

"I need a new school jumper,"
says Rory. He is squashed into his
old jumper. His arms stretch out of
his sleeves like long-necked birds.

"Ah," says Mr O'Connor. "Saint Patrick's School? You have a choice." He shows them two jumpers that look identical. "This one is normal. But this one" – he holds it up – "is amazing. It is expensive, but it won't shrink or wear out. It will last for ever."

"Seriously?" asks Rory.

"Guaranteed," answers Mr O'Connor.

Mammy buys it.

"Now you're all set with uniforms," she says.

"Except I'm wearing my bear cap," whispers Mary.

49

"This jumper lasts for ever,"
says Rory next day in school.

"Nothing lasts for ever," says
Tommy Miller.

"Guaranteed," says Rory. "It won't
shrink or wear out."

"It won't survive red paint," says
Tommy Miller.

Rory paints the jumper.

"Oh, for heaven's sake," says
Mammy. But secretly she is keen to test
the jumper.

The washing-machine water
turns pink.

"You'll have a pink jumper," says
Catherine enviously.

But the jumper drip-dries navy:
perfect.

Rory wears it playing hurling.

It is still perfect.

"But you just stood in goal, reading,"
says Cormac.

"That book is brilliant," says Rory.

"The other team won by miles,"
Cormac tells Anna.

When Rory
puts on the
forever jumper, there is
a moment when he can't see anything.
Inside the forever jumper is like outer
space. Even with his torch,
no light comes through.

"This jumper could
be very useful,"
says Rory.

Every bedtime, Rory brings Jacky upstairs into the boys' room.

Jacky chats loudly, until the lights are off and his cage is covered with a cloth. Then he falls silent. When Rory turns on the lamp to read, light seeps through the cage cover and Jacky scolds and chatters.

"Rory, lights out," calls Daddy.

"Flip," says Rory. He wants to keep reading.

Then Rory tries the forever jumper on Jacky's cage. Jacky falls silent. Rory turns the lamp off and on. Jacky stays silent. Rory reads and reads.

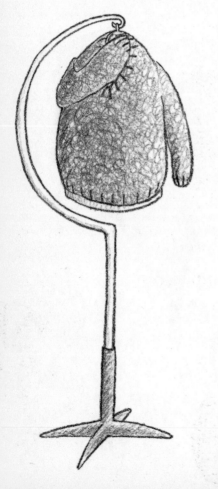

Next day Rory stamps on his jumper in a puddle. It stays perfect.

Next day he snags it in a tree, but the pulled wool springs back. Perfect.

Next day
a hole grows
in the sleeve.

Next day
another hole
pops open
in the tummy.

Soon Rory's white shirt shines
through the forever jumper like
snow at night.

"I'll bring it back to Arnott's," says Mammy, disappointed.

Mr O'Connor is shocked to see the jumper.

"Dreadful!" he gasps. "Please, try another forever jumper. In fact — have two."

"One is plenty," says Mammy.

That night, Daddy and Mammy creep upstairs.

"What's that noise?" whispers Mammy.

"What… Oh, yes," whispers Daddy. "It's from the boys' room."

Mammy and Daddy look inside.

"*Nick-ick-ick,*" goes the noise.

There is Rory, pale and tired and reading another Canadian book.

There is the new jumper over Jacky's cage.

There is Jacky, "*Nick-ick-ick,*" nibbling a hole in it.

Mr O'Connor is not happy to see
Mammy again.

"More holes?" he murmurs anxiously.

"No," says Mammy. "At least,
it wasn't the jumper's fault."

"My budgie nibbled it,"
explains Rory.

"I'd like to pay for the second jumper," says Mammy. "And I'm sorry to have worried you."

But Mr O'Connor is so relieved, he won't let Mammy pay.

The jumper will last until Rory
is squashed into it, then Anna will
have it. Then Mary, then Cormac,
then Catherine. Even Susan,
for a while, will be big
enough to wear the
lasts-forever (if you
don't nibble it)
jumper.